THE DAY DAD JOINED MY SOCCER TEAM

For Fiona K., because she is awesome – M.F.

To my ladies, Katrin and Allister – M.L.

Kids Can Press gratefully acknowledges the financial support of the Government of Ontario, through the Ontario Media Development Corporation; the Ontario Arts Council; the Canada Council for the Arts; and the Government of Canada, through the CBF, for our publishing activity.

Published in Canada and the U.S. by Kids Can Press Ltd.
25 Dockside Drive, Toronto, ON M5A 0B5

Kids Can Press is a Corus Entertainment Inc. company

www.kidscanpress.com

The artwork in this book was rendered in Photoshop.
The text is set in Minya Nouvelle.

Edited by Jennifer Stokes
Designed by Michael Reis

Printed and bound in Malaysia, in 9/2017 by Tien Wah Press (Pte.) Ltd.

CM 18 0 9 8 7 6 5 4 3 2 1

Library and Archives Canada Cataloguing in Publication

Fergus, Maureen, author
    The day Dad joined my soccer team / written by Maureen Fergus ; illustrated by Mike Lowery.

ISBN 978-1-77138-654-8 (hardcover)

I. Lowery, Mike, 1980-, illustrator II. Title.

PS8611.E735D33 2018   jC813'.6   C2017-903210-0

THE DAY DAD JOINED MY SOCCER TEAM

MAUREEN FERGUS
AND MIKE LOWERY

KIDS CAN PRESS

SOCCER

was a ball-kicking,
leg-pumping,
heart-thumping

GOOD TIME.

IT WAS MORE FUN THAN

riding a roller coaster

jumping off a high board

and flying faster-than-fast
down a super-slidey snow hill!

My dad came to all of my games and always cheered louder than anyone, but sometimes I got the feeling that he wanted to do more.

GO TEAM SOCCER DAD

So when Coach said he was looking for a parent volunteer, I told my dad that the team needed his help.

He was so **EXCITED** that he ran right over to the bench, pulled on a jersey and started warming up with the other players.

Before I could explain to Dad that Coach actually wanted him to be in charge of halftime snacks, the referee blew her whistle.

The game was about to start!

We all crowded around Coach to find out what positions he wanted us to play. When my dad heard that he was on defense, he complained that defense was BORING and started whining at Coach to let him play forward instead.

I was embarrassed.

But I was even **MORE** embarrassed when Coach asked us what playing soccer was all about, and my dad shouted,

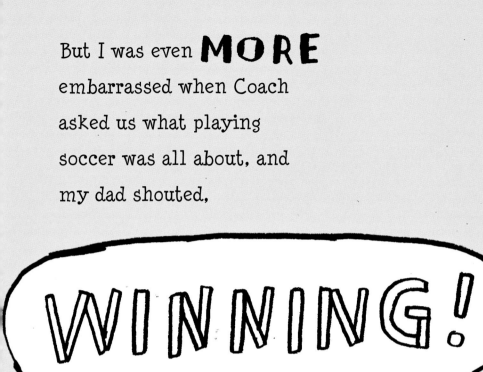

WINNING!

"**DAD**," I whispered, as we jogged onto the field, "playing soccer isn't all about winning."

"It isn't?" he asked in surprise.

"No," I said. "It's all about having fun."

"**GOT IT!**" he said.

But I don't think he **DID** get it because instead of having fun playing soccer, he had fun picking dandelions and waving to the parents and watching airplanes fly by.

And when he was taken off the field for a rest, he had fun fooling around on the sidelines and pestering Coach and kicking the practice balls **EVERYWHERE**.

He even ran off to play in the nearby park!

As I was leading him back to the bench, I explained that the kind of fun he was having wasn't helping the team.

"You need to listen to Coach and **PARTICIPATE**, Dad," I said. "You need to get your head in the game!"

"**GOT IT**," he said.

But I don't think he got that, either, because instead of paying attention and playing his position, he started acting like he was the only one on the field.

And when the other team scored a goal, he groaned as if our goalie had let the ball in **ON PURPOSE**.

Luckily, she didn't notice because everyone else was telling her, "Good try!" and "Don't worry about it!"

I was happy about that — but I sure wasn't happy with my dad.

"You're not being a good sport, Dad!"
I exclaimed.

"How can I be a good sport if we're not winning?" he asked.

Before I could explain that being a good sport meant staying positive, ESPECIALLY when you're not winning, the ball bounced toward us. My dad quickly trapped it and started dribbling up the field.

URGH!

Just as he was about to take a shot on net, a player
on the other team accidentally tripped him.

My dad was **FURIOUS**.
And when the referee
didn't give the other team
a penalty, he threw a
HAIRY FIT!

The referee was much nicer than I would have been. Instead of kicking my dad out of the game, she sent him to the bench to calm down.

"I don't know what we're going to do with him,"
I whispered to Coach. "He's **RUINING** the
game for everyone!"

Coach said that my dad had **ENERGY** and **ENTHUSIASM** and that it was just a matter of pointing him in the right direction.

"If we're patient and keep showing him what it means to be a team player, I'm sure he'll figure it out," he said.

I agreed to keep working with my dad. And I'm glad I did because *YOU KNOW WHAT?* Coach was right!

HOW TO BE A GOOD SPORT

1. PLAY FAIR

2. CHEER FOR YOUR TEAMMATES

3. SHOW RESPECT

4. HAVE FUN!

During the second half, Dad stayed **POSITIVE** and tried hard no matter what the score was or what position Coach asked him to play.

And when he had a chance to try for the winning goal in the final minute of the game, instead of taking the shot himself, he passed the ball to another player: **ME!**

I kicked ... and missed!

And my dad didn't groan a bit! Instead, he gave me a pat on the back and said, "Nice try!"

When the game was over, Dad gave all our players **HIGH FIVES**, thanked the referee for a job well done and offered to collect the corner flags for Coach.

THANKS!

He gave three cheers for the other team and even shook the hand of the player who'd tripped him!

I was so **PROUD**.

"You did **GREAT** today, Dad," I said. "You can play with us anytime."

"Thanks, but some of those kids are a lot tougher than they look," he said as he examined a booboo on his knee. "Maybe there's a less dangerous way for me to help out."

"I heard a rumor that Coach needs a hand with halftime snacks," I said. "Plus, you know, you're really great at cheering, Dad."

Dad said I was a really great person to cheer for, gave me a **BIG HUG** and then squirted me with his water bottle.

As I ducked and ran, I hollered, "I know this is fun, but you really need to get in the car now, Dad. Coach won't take us for slushies until you do!"